Samuel French Acting Edition

I0591772

Luther

by Ethan Lipton

‖ SAMUEL FRENCH ‖

SAMUELFRENCH.COM   **SAMUELFRENCH.CO.UK**

MUSIC USE NOTE

Licensees are solely responsible for obtaining formal written permission from copyright owners to use copyrighted music in the performance of this play and are strongly cautioned to do so. If no such permission is obtained by the licensee, then the licensee must use only original music that the licensee owns and controls. Licensees are solely responsible and liable for all music clearances and shall indemnify the copyright owners of the play(s) and their licensing agent, Samuel French, against any costs, expenses, losses and liabilities arising from the use of music by licensees. Please contact the appropriate music licensing authority in your territory for the rights to any incidental music.

IMPORTANT BILLING AND CREDIT REQUIREMENTS

If you have obtained performance rights to this title, please refer to your licensing agreement for important billing and credit requirements.

LUTHER was first produced by Clubbed Thumb as part of the 17th Annual Summerworks, at HERE Arts Center in June 2012. The performance was directed by Ken Rus Schmoll, with sets by Arnulfo Maldonado, costumes by Jessica Pabst, lighting by Lucrecia Briceno, and sound by Brandon Wolcott. The production stage manager was Mary Spadoni. The cast was as follows:

MARJORIE FORMAN . . . . Kelly Mares

LUTHER SHAW FORMAN. . . . . Bobby Moreno

WALTER FORMAN . . . . Gibson Frazier

TOM / CAPTAIN JAMES . . . . Pete Simpson

MORRIS MCHENRY . . . . .John Ellison Conlee

PHIL / JULIE / OFFICER / SANDY LIEBOWITZ . . . . Crystal Finn

CHARACTERS

MARJORIE FORMAN – a freelancer, early forties
LUTHER SHAW FORMAN – a veteran of war, mid-twenties
WALTER FORMAN – a businessman, mid-forties
TOM – a caterer, early thirties
MORRIS MCHENRY – a stranger, early forties
CAPTAIN JAMES – a policeman, mid-forties
PHIL and **JULIE** – business people, played by puppets
OFFICER – played by a puppet
SANDY LIEBOWITZ – a legal advocate, played by a puppet

SETTING

A world much like ours.

TIME

Soon.

AUTHOR'S NOTES

Tom and Captain James should be played by the same actor. All four puppet characters should be played by one actor (female or male) and those characters should be portrayed with as much gravity and humanity as possible.

Scene One

(A loft that seems to have been built out of a cave. Industrial yet homey, its greatest asset is a window that offers a half-obscured view of a shining, far-away city.)

(On the couch sleeps **LUTHER SHAW FORMAN,** *a scarred, tattooed terrier of a man, bundled up in a blanket.)*

*(***MARJORIE FORMAN,** *a freshly showered genius of early middle age, enters in a bathrobe, toting a bottle of lotion. She sits on the couch at* **LUTHER***'s feet and lathers up her legs.)*

MARJORIE. Walter? Am I wearing my black dress with the notches in the sleeves, or the green wraparound?

WALTER. *(Offstage.)* Oh. I like both of those dresses.

MARJORIE. Maybe the green one.

WALTER. *(Offstage.)* Yeah, wear the green one. It's very approachable, that one.

(Enter **WALTER FORMAN,** *a charmer with a recent paunch, wrestling his tie.)*

(The tie.) Is this thing too smudgy?

MARJORIE. I can't see without my glasses.

*(***WALTER** *moves in closer.)*

Meh.

WALTER. Nobody's going to notice that.

MARJORIE. Who cares if they do?

WALTER. I'm wearing it.

MARJORIE. *(After a moment.)* Honey?

WALTER. Yeah?

MARJORIE. I think Luther would like to come with us to the party tonight.

WALTER. *(Skipping that.)* Did you ask your brother about watching him when we go out of town?

MARJORIE. Oh, yeah, he can't do it.

WALTER. What?

MARJORIE. His in-laws are going to be here that same week.

WALTER. *(Devastated.)* Oh god.

MARJORIE. Sucks, huh?

WALTER. When did you find this out?

MARJORIE. Yesterday, when I talked to Billy.

WALTER. You just talked to Billy yesterday?

MARJORIE. Do you still want me to ask Rick and Jessica?

WALTER. We can't ask Rick and Jessica now. We leave in eight days.

MARJORIE. So?

WALTER. So we barely know them, it's rude. If we wanted to ask them, we should have done it weeks ago.

MARJORIE. Well, but we didn't.

WALTER. Because you said you'd rather ask your brother first.

MARJORIE. Which is what I did.

> *(Dreaming on the couch,* **LUTHER** *endures a sort of huffing tremor.* **WALTER** *takes off his tie, mangles it.)*

Why did you say Rick and Jessica would be a good backup if you never intended to use them?

WALTER. Rick and Jessica would be a good backup assuming we could give them some notice. It's not like one of us got hit by a car.

MARJORIE. I could not have less of an idea what that means.

WALTER. It's not an emergency. You've been talking about taking this vacation for years. We can't call up Rick and Jessica now and say, "Hey guys, sorry but we just got attacked by a sudden trip to Cava Lupé, can you bail us out?"

MARJORIE. *(An old wound.)* There is nothing morally wrong with wanting to take a vacation.

WALTER. That's not what I'm saying.

MARJORIE. If we lived in a civilized society where eighty percent of our income didn't go to rent, we might even take one every decade –

WALTER. Honey?

MARJORIE. I am so tired of you trying to make me feel bad for wanting to go away with my husband for one fucking week of my life.

WALTER. I wasn't trying to make you feel bad –

MARJORIE. Oh, that was you making me feel good?

WALTER. – For wanting to go on vacation! I was trying to make you feel bad for not calling your brother three weeks ago, when you said you were going to do it! And I'm sorry.

MARJORIE. Maybe I shouldn't go tonight.

WALTER. Marjorie –

MARJORIE. I mean, I never cared about your stupid work party to begin with, but I really don't care about it now, after you make me feel like crap for not having called my brother six months in advance? When I have been...? It's a lot, Walter.

(Re: everything at home.)

This is a lot.

WALTER. *(Sympathetic.)* I know.

MARJORIE. I called Billy as soon as I got the chance.

WALTER. I know.

MARJORIE. Do you know I haven't left the apartment in two days just trying to finish all these fucking fuckaloo projects?

WALTER. No, I didn't. But I should have.

(Going to her.)

WALTER. See, this is why I can't come home after work if we're going to go out for the night, because as soon as I get on that train, all the blood rushes out of my head and I turn into a total moron, and by the time I walk through the door all I want to do is crawl into bed.

MARJORIE. And that would be so terrible?

WALTER. No.

> (**WALTER** *takes her hand and rests his forehead against hers.*)

MARJORIE. *(With love.)* You smell hungry.

WALTER. I am.

MARJORIE. What'd you have for lunch?

WALTER. Turkey sandwich.

MARJORIE. That's it?

WALTER. I thought about getting some pretzels. Just couldn't decide which ones. What about you guys?

MARJORIE. Cereal, with yogurt and blueberries.

WALTER. And?

MARJORIE. I was so busy working, and Lu said he wasn't that hungry.

WALTER. Okay, but honey, you guys have to eat more than cereal and yogurt.

MARJORIE. I know.

WALTER. How was he today?

MARJORIE. Good. Spent most of the morning reading. Did his treadmill and his rope.

WALTER. Nice.

MARJORIE. Worked on his puzzle, we did that together.

WALTER. How's his skin?

MARJORIE. Better. Still itchy, but not so inflamed.

> *(After a moment.)*

Why do you want me to go to this thing?

WALTER. Because A – it's at the corporate estate, which is supposed to be super weird. And B – it might be fun.

MARJORIE. You think of those people as being fun?

WALTER. Yeah, in a worky kind of way.

MARJORIE. Maybe we shouldn't be together anymore.

WALTER. Oh, Jesus fucking Christ, Marjorie.

MARJORIE. I'm serious, we don't even like the same kinds of people.

WALTER. We do so like the same kinds of people!

(**LUTHER** *groans in his sleep.*)

Case in point. And just so you know, those people, who you think are so awful, all happen to like you very much.

MARJORIE. I didn't say they were awful. I just get bored always being the one in charge of...curiosity. None of them ever asks me about myself. Not that I'd have anything to say, but it might be nice to be asked.

WALTER. They don't ask you about yourself because you are smart and beautiful, and they are nervous and insecure.

MARJORIE. Right.

WALTER. Most people are nervous and insecure. We're two of our favorite people, and we get nervous and insecure thirty times a day. But if you know that about people and you try to help them overcome it, and everyone is helping each other out with their nervous insecurity, then there's a chance for something kind and generous and wonderful to happen between people.

MARJORIE. Maybe Billy's in-laws can stay with Lu when they come to town.

WALTER. (*This changes everything.*) Maybe that's the most ingenious idea I've ever heard.

MARJORIE. You think?

WALTER. Yes! Billy's in-laws are crazy about Luther. Don't you remember at Thanksgiving, Fred and Luther were playing chess all day? They couldn't get enough of each other. And Fred said he'd always wanted to adopt a soldier, they just didn't allow it in their building.

MARJORIE. That is so disgusting to me.

WALTER. It shouldn't even be legal.

MARJORIE. I'm going to find out the name of their landlord and start crank-calling that son of a bitch –

WALTER. Okay, but can we wait until after they watch Luther for the week?

MARJORIE. I'll run it by Billy in the morning.

WALTER. Excellent! See that? Everything's going to work out perfectly.

MARJORIE. Really. Even though we didn't plan it all a year in advance?

WALTER. I know, technically such a thing shouldn't be possible, but somehow, this time, it may work out.

MARJORIE. This time, or most times?

WALTER. No, most times I do the planning and no one has to worry.

MARJORIE. Right, because you don't worry when you do the planning.

WALTER. I worry less.

MARJORIE. What do you think would happen if you tried not to worry at all?

WALTER. Sadly, I would burst into flames.

MARJORIE. All right, let me put on some clothes.

(**MARJORIE** *goes off to the bedroom.*)

WALTER. Thank you, honey. For calling Billy, and for going with me tonight. I really appreciate it.

MARJORIE. *(Offstage.)* You're welcome. And thank you for letting me bring Luther to the party.

(**LUTHER** *has another tremor.*)

WALTER. Marjorie? Do you really think that's a good idea?

MARJORIE. *(Offstage.)* Yes. The poor guy's dying to go out. And he's been so good lately, he really has been a perfect gentleman.

(**MARJORIE** *returns, wearing the black dress with notches.*)

And I think he deserves it. Don't you?

WALTER. I mean, I would give him the world if we could. I'm just not sure it's about deserving.

MARJORIE. Well, I am. Besides, he loves parties.

WALTER. I don't think he loves parties.

MARJORIE. He loves our parties.

WALTER. Here, small gathering, with people he knows.

MARJORIE. We never let him do anything, Walter.

WALTER. Because we discovered he's psychotically oversensitive. That's why we came up with that policy.

MARJORIE. No, we came up with that policy because he *was* psychotically oversensitive. We have no idea what he'd be like if we took him out because it's been so long since we tried. It's like we punish him now for having been unpredictable then; like we decided he'd stay that way forever, when the truth is he has changed, in so many ways.

WALTER. Yeah, but –

MARJORIE. When we first brought him home he wouldn't even eat with us. He never slept when we were here. He wouldn't look you in the eye for the first six months; now he's madly in love with you. I just wonder if maybe he needs our encouragement, in addition to our... concern.

WALTER. And, so, if he went, how would that work, I'd watch him?

MARJORIE. Or I will, I don't mind.

WALTER. But you're the one who never gets to socialize.

MARJORIE. I'll be socializing with Luther, we'll do it together. If he wants to go. If he doesn't want to, he doesn't have to. Only if he wants to.

WALTER. It would be nice if we could go out now and then as a family.

MARJORIE. Wouldn't it?

WALTER. Luther? Hey, buddy?

MARJORIE. Wait.

(MARJORIE squirts lotion onto her hands, then, sneaking her hands up the leg of LUTHER's pants, rubs some into his calves.)

WALTER. Don't scare him.

MARJORIE. Shhh, he loves it.

(LUTHER twitches, then begins to enjoy it. WALTER gets some lotion and joins MARJORIE, each one lathering up a leg.)

LUTHER. Fuh-fuh-fuh-fuh...

(So pleased is the still-sleeping LUTHER that he turns over and begins rubbing their hands with his head.)

MARJORIE. Luther? Luther?

LUTHER. *(Opening his eyes.)* Mm-hm?

MARJORIE. Would you like to go with us to the party tonight?

LUTHER. Yeah. That'd be nice.

Scene Two

(The corporate estate: a hi-tech combination of Sheboygan and Boca Raton. A good time threatens to break out at any moment.)

*(**MARJORIE** and **LUTHER** take in the scene, **LUTHER** now looking sharp in a suit. He chews gum. Both drink wine.)*

MARJORIE. Can you believe this place?

LUTHER. It reminds me of a palace.

MARJORIE. Or a dollhouse. Have you ever seen anything so tacky?

LUTHER. Oh, uh...no.

MARJORIE. And look at these people. Where do they come from?

LUTHER. Where?

MARJORIE. No, I mean, how did they get here? In life? Is this what they were hoping for? Is this what they wanted it all to add up to?

LUTHER. Yes.

MARJORIE. It is, isn't it?

LUTHER. This is just what they wanted.

MARJORIE. *(Toasting.)* To them and their domination of our world.

(They clink glasses and drink.)

LUTHER. Where did you put your gum?

*(**MARJORIE** holds out her hand. **LUTHER** drops his gum into it, straight from his mouth.)*

MARJORIE. What kind of palace? You said it reminded you of a palace?

LUTHER. Yeah. One that I stayed in during the war.

MARJORIE. So this was a real palace.

LUTHER. Yeah.

MARJORIE. I thought it might be a made-up palace.

LUTHER. No.

MARJORIE. And what was it like, this palace?

LUTHER. Old. And big. Maybe twice as big as this place. Every room had a canopy over the bed, and a view of the river. It was built right next to a river, and every room had a view. At night, when the stars were shining, you could see their reflection in the water.

MARJORIE. It sounds lovely.

LUTHER. It was.

MARJORIE. I didn't know they let the soldiers stay in palaces.

LUTHER. Well, we sort of insisted.

(**LUTHER** *finishes his drink in a gulp.*)

MARJORIE. (*Suddenly worried for him.*) Should we...is this weird? Being here? Do you want to go home?

LUTHER. Why?

MARJORIE. So you don't have to deal with all these people.

LUTHER. What's wrong with them?

MARJORIE. Well, they're crazy, for one.

LUTHER. What makes you say that?

MARJORIE. I've talked to them.

LUTHER. Not since we got here.

MARJORIE. At other events, okay? And believe me, there's always a price to pay.

LUTHER. What kind of a price?

MARJORIE. Boredom. Condescension. Nausea.

LUTHER. People can't make you nauseous.

MARJORIE. Take a whiff. Go on, take a whiff, tell me what you smell.

(**LUTHER** *inhales.*)

LUTHER. Is that pork?

MARJORIE. Yes. And do you know where it's coming from?

LUTHER. The appetizers?

MARJORIE. The people.

LUTHER. Come on.

MARJORIE. That's what they're wearing. It's like, all the rage these days.

LUTHER. That's crazy.

MARJORIE. That's what I'm saying, okay? We don't want to be here, do we?

LUTHER. Would you like to go home?

MARJORIE. It's too much, right?

LUTHER. I like it.

MARJORIE. No you don't.

LUTHER. It makes everyone seem more human.

MARJORIE. It's pork, Luther. They're pig people.

LUTHER. *(Trying to read her needs.)* Let's go home.

MARJORIE. Are you sure?

LUTHER. Yeah, I was just as worried about dealing with these crazy people as you were.

MARJORIE. Worried? Wait, worried? I wasn't worried.

I was disinterested maybe, and nauseous. Were you worried? Why were you worried?

LUTHER. I mean, honestly, I haven't been around this many strangers in years. How would I even know what to say?

MARJORIE. Well, look, all you do...all you do is ask them how they're doing. Or *what* they're doing, even better, they all love to talk about what they do. And then if you start to get nervous, you just remind yourself that they're just as nervous and insecure as you are. And you try to help them. You be your kind, wonderful, loving self, and you be there for them.

LUTHER. You do it.

MARJORIE. I have done it, many times.

LUTHER. But you can't do it anymore?

MARJORIE. No, of course I can.

LUTHER. So do it.

MARJORIE. You do it.

LUTHER. Can I? Go up and talk to somebody.

MARJORIE. By yourself?

LUTHER. Yeah. And you do it too, but with somebody else, and then we meet up later to debrief.

MARJORIE. *(Mustering the courage.)* Okay. Pick somebody.

> (**LUTHER** *and* **MARJORIE** *survey the partygoers. Suddenly,* **LUTHER** *starts to walk off, but* **MARJORIE** *grabs hold of him.)*

Don't just walk off without saying goodbye, for god's sake. Now, where are you going?

LUTHER. Over there.

MARJORIE. Where?

LUTHER. By the fountain.

MARJORIE. Okay. I'll be...next to the food.

LUTHER. Okay. I'll be by the fountain.

> (**MARJORIE** *pushes him away and* **LUTHER** *exits. She watches him go, takes a breath, then exits in the other direction.)*

> (**WALTER** *enters, chatting with a pair of puppets: co-workers* **PHIL** *and* **JULIE**.*)*

PHIL. Walter, you're absolutely right.

JULIE. I'm going to try it in my department too.

PHIL. Why didn't I think of it sooner?

JULIE. Because you were too busy banging your head against the wall.

WALTER. Well, listen, Phil, there aren't too many guarantees in this world –

PHIL. That's so true!

WALTER. But the way I see it –

PHIL. I know!

WALTER. Know what?

PHIL. Sorry, I cut you off. Go on?

WALTER. Oh, well, all I was going to say is, the way I see it, you don't have much to lose.

PHIL. Yes.

JULIE. Poetry!

PHIL. That does it, I'm emailing all of my people tonight.

JULIE. Walter, when are you going to get promoted already?

PHIL. Screw the promotion, they ought to name a holiday after this guy!

> (**JULIE** *and* **PHIL** *laugh.* **WALTER** *scans the room, looking a little bored.*)

JULIE. Who needs another drink?

WALTER. Oh, I guess.

JULIE. Great.

PHIL. Now, tell me about this thing you're doing with spreadsheets.

> (**WALTER** *exits with* **PHIL** *and* **JULIE.**)

> (*By the kitchen,* **LUTHER** *approaches* **TOM***, a caterer, and takes a glass of wine from the tray he is holding.*)

LUTHER. Do you mind?

TOM. That's what they're here for.

LUTHER. *(Clears his throat.)* So what do you do?

TOM. I'm a doctor.

LUTHER. Really?

TOM. That's right.

LUTHER. What kind of medicine do you practice?

TOM. Caterology.

LUTHER. I'm not familiar with that.

TOM. It's the practice of catering.

LUTHER. Sounds like a pretty specialized field.

TOM. Yeah, it's special all right. Some of the kitchen guys like to call me the special caterer. Can I take your glass?

> (**TOM** *takes* **LUTHER***'s empty glass.*)

LUTHER. Well done.

TOM. I'm a professional.

> (*After a moment.*)

TOM. I'm also a painter.

LUTHER. Nice. What kind of painting do you like to do?

TOM. Oh, did I say I like painting? I don't like painting.

LUTHER. I'm sorry.

TOM. I paint because I have to.

LUTHER. Because somebody makes you?

TOM. Yeah, I make me.

> (**LUTHER** *gives* **TOM** *a big, firm hug.*)

What are you doing? –

> (**TOM** *relaxes into it. Finally,* **LUTHER** *lets him go. It's quiet.*)

LUTHER. There are some beautiful women here.

TOM. Right.

LUTHER. Which one would you choose if you could pick one?

TOM. I don't know. I...

LUTHER. I'd choose that woman in the purple dress, that V-back thing? Or Marjorie.

TOM. Marjorie?

LUTHER. See the one talking to the big man there?

TOM. Oh, yeah. She a friend of yours?

LUTHER. Yeah. She's a great friend.

> (**LUTHER** *finishes his wine, sets it on the tray, takes another.* **TOM** *assays the room.*)

TOM. I like the pale one over there with the dark orange hair.

LUTHER. She's beautiful too.

TOM. Isn't she though?

> (*Elsewhere,* **MARJORIE** *is talking to* **MORRIS MCHENRY**, *a big man who eats tidily from a plate of appetizers.*)

MARJORIE. And how is that, being a senior business operations supervisor?

MORRIS. Oh, it suits me, I guess. Sometimes I wonder.

MARJORIE. Yes?

MORRIS. What it would be like. You know, to do something else?

MARJORIE. Really? What? If you could do anything in the world, what would it be?

MORRIS. Well, I wouldn't mind being Daren Davis.

MARJORIE. Who is...?

MORRIS. Vice president of operations.

(**MORRIS** *continues eating.*)

I used to be in publishing.

MARJORIE. Oh?

MORRIS. Yeah, but I hurt my back.

MARJORIE. While you were working?

MORRIS. Doing laundry. Now I have to have someone pick it up for me. My doctor says I shouldn't even be folding it.

MARJORIE. I have a friend who teaches pilates –

MORRIS. Have you ever had shingles?

MARJORIE. No. I never have had shingles.

MORRIS. My god, that was the worst. So embarrassing.

MARJORIE. Embarrassing?

MORRIS. Because don't you think it's for old people? When you think about shingles?

MARJORIE. I don't think about it too often.

MORRIS. Well, it's not. Anyone can get it. And it's really scary if you do. I thought I was going to die.

MARJORIE. That's awful. I'm so sorry.

MORRIS. I had a lot of cold sores when I was a kid.

MARJORIE. Uh-huh?

MORRIS. People used to make fun of me. Somewhat viciously, if you want to know the truth. But I would rather get a million cold sores than have to go through shingles again.

MARJORIE. Well, that definitely says something.

MORRIS. Would you like to try a tuna tartare?

MARJORIE. Oh, no thank you.

MORRIS. They're delicious.

MARJORIE. I already ate.

MORRIS. Just try one.

MARJORIE. Really, I can't.

MORRIS. *(After a moment.)* I like you, Marjorie.

MARJORIE. I like you too, Mr. McHenry.

MORRIS. *(Stung.)* Morris.

MARJORIE. Yes, yes, I'm sorry, Morris.

MORRIS. God.

MARJORIE. I didn't mean anything by it.

MORRIS. It doesn't matter. Damn it. Ach.

> *(Guilt-ridden,* **MARJORIE** *reaches for his plate.)*

MARJORIE. Maybe I will try one –

MORRIS. Oh, here.

> *(***MORRIS** *offers to feed* **MARJORIE***, and before she can stop him, his fingers are in her mouth.)*

Isn't it yummy?

MARJORIE. *(In shock/terror.)* Mmm!

MORRIS. Let's go get some more before they run out.

> *(***MORRIS** *takes* **MARJORIE***'s hand and leads her off.)*
>
> *(By the kitchen,* **TOM** *is now drinking wine too.* **LUTHER** *holds another full glass of wine and is well on his way to loopy.)*

TOM. So how'd you end up working with these goofballs?

LUTHER. Oh, I don't work with them, Tom. I live with them.

TOM. Must be a big apartment.

LUTHER. Ha! Not everybody. Just Walter and Marjorie.

TOM. Ah, yes, the lovely Marjorie. And here she comes.

> *(***TOM** *points to* **MARJORIE***, who's walking toward them.)*

> *(Before she can reach them:)*

LUTHER. *(Warding her off.)* I'm not done yet.

> **(MARJORIE** *stops in her tracks. She turns around, where* **MORRIS** *awaits her attention.)*

MORRIS. I thought I had lost you.

MARJORIE. No.

> **(MARJORIE** *walks off, with* **MORRIS** *right on her heels.)*

LUTHER. She's practicing having fun.

TOM. And you live with her?

LUTHER. Yeah.

TOM. And her husband.

LUTHER. Walter, yeah, he's the best.

TOM. What do you do for a living, Luther?

LUTHER. I'm retired.

TOM. Trust fund?

LUTHER. Nope.

TOM. Technology? Or wait, the market? Were you a stockbroker, Luther?

LUTHER. I was in the service.

TOM. In the war?

LUTHER. Yeah.

TOM. For how long?

LUTHER. Uh…six years.

TOM. *(Starstruck.)* That's awesome!

LUTHER. Yeah?

TOM. Luther, do you know what you are?

LUTHER. Drunk?

TOM. Dude, you're a fucking hero.

LUTHER. Uh…

TOM. Yes you are, a man of action at sea in an ocean of cowards.

LUTHER. That's not really what it's like –

TOM. What have we ever done with our lives, huh? Me? What have I ever done for anyone else?

LUTHER. Lots, I'm sure.

TOM. Nothing! I haven't done shit, man. I never volunteered or joined a cause. All I do is make shit up in my imagination and pretend that it means something. But you, you have literally made the world a better place.

LUTHER. Uh-huh?

TOM. You have lessened the evil and increased the good.

LUTHER. *(A panic attack.)* I feel a little bit warm –

TOM. Did you get some of those fuckers?

LUTHER. Who – what?

TOM. Tell me you got some of those fuckers.

LUTHER. I did, yeah –

TOM. How many?

LUTHER. Some, I got some.

TOM. More than ten?

LUTHER. I'm going to get some fresh air on the beach –

TOM. And that scar, did you get that in battle?

> (**LUTHER** *huffs, trying to catch his breath, and exits quickly.*)

Hey, I want to paint you!

> (*Elsewhere,* **WALTER** *chats with* **PHIL** *and* **JULIE.**)

WALTER. ...But I had meant to send it to myself and BCC.

> (**JULIE** *and* **PHIL** *explode in laughter.*)

JULIE. That's the craziest thing I ever heard!

PHIL. Oh, Jesus, Walter! You kill me!

JULIE. Walter, Walter, Walter.

WALTER. Yeah, well...

PHIL. Walter, Walter, Walter, Walter!

WALTER. You guys.

JULIE. No, you!

PHIL. You! You, you, you, you, you!

> *(From far away, a scream is heard.)*

WALTER. Have either of you seen Luther?

PHIL. Luther's here?

JULIE. You brought him?

WALTER. Yeah, well, he's been doing so well lately –

PHIL. I got to talk to that guy.

JULIE. Walter, that's fabulous.

PHIL. Where is he?

WALTER. I don't know exactly.

PHIL. Come on, where is he?

WALTER. I don't know.

JULIE. You're such a good person, Walter. How come I can't meet a man like you?

WALTER. I'm sorry?

JULIE. All I ever meet are assholes and junkies.

WALTER. Well, geez, Julie –

PHIL. Where did you leave him, Walter, do you remember?

WALTER. With Marjorie.

PHIL. And where's she, do you want me to find her?

WALTER. I...excuse me.

> *(**WALTER** runs offstage.)*
>
> *(**PHIL** starts to go off after him, but **JULIE** stops him.)*

JULIE. Would you get a hold of yourself?

PHIL. What?

JULIE. You're fawning all over him. Give the guy some space.

PHIL. I thought we were trying to win points.

JULIE. There's a difference between flattery and fellatio, Phil. Now come on, let's go see if Ellsberry has any coke.

> *(They exit.)*

(Elsewhere, upstairs, MORRIS leads MARJORIE into a room where loud music is playing. He moves a short distance away from her and bobs his head to the beat, listening.)*

MARJORIE. I should go find my family.

MORRIS. Just a second.

MARJORIE. No one else is dancing.

MORRIS. Somebody has to start it. I love this song.

MARJORIE. Morris –

MORRIS. And...now!

(MORRIS begins to dance. MORRIS is an amazing dancer.)

MARJORIE. Morris! You're an amazing dancer!

MORRIS. *(In one breath.)* My doctor asked if I get any exercise I said no but I like to dance he said keep dancing!

(Despite herself, MARJORIE begins to dance. She too is a great dancer.)

MARJORIE. How come nobody dances at parties anymore?

MORRIS. It gets in the way of phony conversation.

(MORRIS shows off an interesting series of tiny moves.)

MARJORIE. What's that?

MORRIS. The small dance.

MARJORIE. It's very nice.

MORRIS. I invented it.

(MARJORIE shows off some punchy moves.)

MARJORIE. Are you familiar with this?

MORRIS. Boxer dance.

---

*A license to produce *Luther* does not include a performance license for any third-party or copyrighted music. Licensees should create an original composition or use music in the public domain. For further information, please see Music Use Note on page 3.

MARJORIE. Yeah!

MORRIS. How about Texan boxer dance?

> (**MARJORIE** and **MORRIS** really enjoy dancing together.)

MARJORIE. I never get to dance!

MORRIS. Everybody gets to dance!

> (Outside the party, on the beach, **WALTER** tries to catch **LUTHER**, who runs past him in nothing but his underwear.)

WALTER. Luther? Luther, please come over here.

LUTHER. (Offstage.) You have to catch me.

WALTER. God dammit, Luther! You get your butt over here and put your clothes on right now!

> (**LUTHER** enters, walks up to **WALTER**.)

LUTHER. I'm sorry...that you are not as fast as I.

> (**LUTHER** jukes, fakes, and runs offstage, leaving **WALTER** empty-handed.)

WALTER. Luther!

> (After a long moment **LUTHER** enters, sprinting...)

LUTHER. Hey, Walter, how's it going?

> (...And exits sprinting as **WALTER** dives after him, catching nothing but sand.)

WALTER. Boy, you are in trouble. You are in big, big trouble.

LUTHER. (Offstage.) Fuck you!

WALTER. What did you just say?

LUTHER. (Offstage.) What did you just say?

WALTER. (Reining it in.) Okay. Okay, buddy, you win! You are the champion, okay?

LUTHER. (Offstage.) Good game.

WALTER. Good game, good game.

LUTHER. (Offstage.) Rematch.

WALTER. No! Buddy, listen, I'm gassed, okay? I got nothing in the tank.

> *(A moment.)*

Luther? Can I tell you a secret?

LUTHER. *(Offstage.)* What?

WALTER. Come here for a second.

LUTHER. *(Offstage.)* What's the secret?

WALTER. Come here and I'll tell you.

> **(LUTHER** *enters, keeping a bit of distance.)*

I love you.

LUTHER. That's not a secret.

WALTER. I know. And the secret is: I got you a present. Peanut butter and chocolate ice cream. I brought it home last night and snuck it into the freezer. And if you put your clothes on right now and go back inside to the party with me, you can have some when we get home. How does that sound?

> **(WALTER** *lunges at* **LUTHER,** *grabbing him around the midsection, and this time* **LUTHER** *lets himself get caught.)*

Ya-ha! Not as slow as you thought, am I?

LUTHER. I already had some ice cream.

WALTER. You ate my ice cream?

LUTHER. Marjorie and I had it for lunch.

WALTER. I could kill you.

> *(With frightening speed,* **LUTHER** *clutches* **WALTER***'s neck and brings him to his knees.)*

Oh-ho-ho!

LUTHER. Could you, Walter? How would you do it?

WALTER. Luther!

LUTHER. How would you kill me?

WALTER. Buddy, please, I would never hurt you.

> **(LUTHER** *releases* **WALTER,** *who falls back onto the sand face-up, catching his breath.)*

(LUTHER lays his body across WALTER's, crushing him with a hug.)

LUTHER. I would never hurt you, Walter.

(Exhausted, relieved, WALTER returns the embrace. It's quiet. The waves crash.)

(LUTHER looks up at the ocean, alarmed.)

(Stealthily.) Look out.

WALTER. What?

LUTHER. Something in the water.

WALTER. Ships or people?

LUTHER. Seaweed.

WALTER. What's it doing?

LUTHER. Mobilizing.

WALTER. Hey, should we go back inside?

LUTHER. Don't move.

(LUTHER bolts up and sprints off toward the ocean.)

WALTER. Luther!

(On the balcony, MARJORIE and MORRIS smoke cigarettes, drunk. Behind them we see glimpses of a now-bustling dance floor. Perhaps JULIE and PHIL are dancing.)

MORRIS. So how do you balance the needs of your family with the needs of your job and still find time for yourself?

MARJORIE. Where have you been all my life?

MORRIS. Well, I grew up in Michigan.

MARJORIE. If I want to find time for myself, Morris, I have to make an appointment. And then, if something comes up – and something always comes up – who do you think is the first person I cancel on?

MORRIS. Marjorie Elizabeth Forman.

MARJORIE. That's right. Because I have no respect for my own pleasure.

MORRIS. You should get some.

MARJORIE. I should!

MORRIS. Well, I guess you get the pleasure of being your own boss.

>   (**MARJORIE** *begins to cry.*)

You don't like freelancing?

MARJORIE. Morris, if the man who invented freelancing walked into this party, I'd punch him in the neck. Free? Where is the free in never knowing when your next job will come? Where is the free when every day feels like Monday? When the weekend is nothing but a chance to catch up on all the work you failed to finish on all the Mondays that came before it?

Where is the free when you can't take an hour's lunch break because you the employee are terrified of what you the employer might say? When you the employer can never be satisfied, and not just with the volume of work, because there's never enough, but with the quality, Morris, the sad-sack piss-poor quality. When every project you finish underwhelms you and you're always thinking that if you were just that much more business savvy or detail-oriented, you might have done better. Where is the free when you have to hold on to every fucking receipt you ever get so you can claim that every purchase you ever make is in service of your job? Which isn't even true. It isn't true, Morris! You just feel like it ought to be true.

MORRIS. Maybe you could fire yourself and go on unemployment.

MARJORIE. *(Laughs.)* I don't think it works that way. But thank you for asking.

>   (*Seated on the sand,* **LUTHER** *pops seaweed pods, one after the next, as if he were assassinating them.* **WALTER** *helps.*)

WALTER. Maybe we do this for five more minutes and then we go back inside?

LUTHER. When did you know you were in love with Marjorie?

WALTER. Did you hear me?

LUTHER. Yes, I heard you.

WALTER. A long time ago.

LUTHER. At the picnic?

WALTER. After that.

LUTHER. Did you bring anything to the picnic?

WALTER. I brought a tabouli salad. And a couple of baseball gloves and a ball.

LUTHER. *(Re: the seaweed.)* Make sure you do that whole section. It'll send an important message. How come you never make us tabouli salad?

WALTER. I think I discovered it makes me burpy.

LUTHER. You know what makes me burpy?

WALTER. What?

> *(**LUTHER** burps.)*

Nice.

> *(**LUTHER** burps again.)*

Did you know you have a – *(Burps.)*
On your – *(Burps.)*?

> *(**LUTHER** burps affirmatively.)*
>
> *(The scenes continue on both the balcony and the beach.)*

MARJORIE. I never cared much for soldiers.

MORRIS. Me neither.

MARJORIE. Or cops – I'm sort of allergic to cops. But soldiers always scared me. The look in their eyes.

LUTHER. What did Marjorie bring to the picnic?

WALTER. I'll give you three guesses.

LUTHER. Crispy fried chicken.

MARJORIE. But the moment I saw Luther, I was like, that's my boy. That's my family. And Walter felt the same.

LUTHER. Is that when you knew you loved her? You tasted her fried chicken and you were like, I got to be with this lady?

MARJORIE. You could just tell there was someone special inside.

WALTER. No. I thought she was cute, but she wasn't overly friendly.

MARJORIE. Not that he was all warm and cuddly at first.

WALTER. She made fun of my baseball cap five minutes after we met. Said she could smell it from where she was sitting. Plus, she was still getting over some doofy ex-boyfriend.

MARJORIE. He was dark. And sort of far away, as if, when you were talking to him he was still in the other room.

LUTHER. How long did it take you to kiss her?

WALTER. Two dates.

MARJORIE. It was freezing, I remember, and the only thing Luther said to us that whole first day was, "You better have heat."

MORRIS. And what'd you say?

MARJORIE. I said, "We do."

WALTER. We went to see a Charlie Chaplin movie downtown. And at some point, the backs of our forearms started brushing up against each other on the armrests.

MARJORIE. They give you this long, yellow printout, before you sign the adoption papers. It's a profile, a list of all the things that have happened to him, and everything he's ever done.

WALTER. I took her to Rocco's for dinner, and then I walked her back to her bus stop, and that's when I gave her the smooch.

MARJORIE. They handed the profile to Walter, and we looked at each other, and without either one of us saying a word, he folded it up and put it away in his pocket.

MORRIS. You never read it?

MARJORIE. We didn't want to know. We didn't need to.

WALTER. When the bus pulled up to take her home, I'll never forget, she pushed me away. Gave me a big shove, with a smile on her face.

LUTHER. Did you pay for dinner?

WALTER. Yes, I paid for dinner.

LUTHER. Just asking.

MARJORIE. *(Starting to feel dizzy.)* I think I've had too much to drink.

MORRIS. That's okay.

MARJORIE. No –

> (**MARJORIE** *is about to throw up when* **MORRIS** *guides her to a nearby planter. He looks around for help, then decides, out of an urge to comfort, to sing to her as she retches:*)

MORRIS.
> THIS OLD MAN, HE PLAYED ONE
> HE PLAYED KNICK-KNACK ON MY THUMB
> WITH A KNICK-KNACK-PADDY-WHACK
> GIVE A DOG A BONE
> THIS OLD MAN CAME ROLLING HOME

> THIS OLD MAN, HE PLAYED TWO...

> (**MORRIS** *continues to sing as* **LUTHER** *and* **WALTER** *keep popping seaweed pods.*)

WALTER. Why wouldn't I pay?

LUTHER. I thought maybe you went dutch.

WALTER. No, I paid.

LUTHER. Sometimes you seem like you're just putting up with things.

WALTER. What does that mean?

LUTHER. I don't know.

WALTER. Well then why would you say it?

LUTHER. I don't know.

WALTER. You know, you're not the only one here with feelings.

LUTHER. I know.

WALTER. I am not just putting up with things. Ever. I'm trying to make things better.

LUTHER. Okay.

WALTER. At my job, I'm very well-respected for just that quality, for trying to improve things in any way I can. It's something I work very hard at.

LUTHER. If you're so well-respected, how come you don't make more money?

WALTER. I make as much money as I'm supposed to. This city is very expensive. If we lived somewhere else, if we lived in Mississippi, for example, we'd be upper middle class.

LUTHER. Would we have a backyard?

WALTER. Yes, we'd have a backyard and an attic and a basement, and probably a front porch too.

LUTHER. So what are we doing living here?

WALTER. Don't push me, Luther. Okay? I am looking you in the eye, man to man, and I'm asking you: Do not push me.

LUTHER. Which one of us do you think Marjorie loves more?

WALTER. All right, that's it.

(**WALTER** *stands.*)

LUTHER. What?

WALTER. You want to play this game, you can do it alone.

LUTHER. Where are you going?

WALTER. I'm sorry that we brought you to the party.

LUTHER. What did I do?

WALTER. I'm sorry if it stressed you out or got you upset –

LUTHER. I'm not upset –

WALTER. Or overstimulated or whatever –

LUTHER. It didn't overstimulate me! It made me happy! To see all these things?! I never get to see these things! I like it! This is fun!

WALTER. You need to take a deep breath.

LUTHER. No, you need to sit down and help me finish this seaweed.

WALTER. I'm not going to help you finish the seaweed –

LUTHER. Yes you are!

WALTER. Luther?

LUTHER. Walter?

> *(On the balcony,* **MARJORIE** *has stopped retching.)*

MORRIS. Better?

> *(***MARJORIE** *resumes retching.)*

THIS OLD MAN, HE PLAYED FIVE...

> *(On the beach:)*

WALTER. I am going back into that house, and I'm going to get our stuff and I'm going to find Marjorie, and we are going to go home.

LUTHER. I didn't mean to make you angry.

WALTER. It's too late for that.

LUTHER. But I don't want to go.

WALTER. And sadly that's not your choice anymore.

LUTHER. I promise to only say complimentary things.

WALTER. You're out of control.

LUTHER. No I'm not!

WALTER. I asked you before, and what did you say –

LUTHER. But I didn't promise! I didn't promise before, now I am promising.

WALTER. Do you want me to call the police?

LUTHER. What?

WALTER. I don't know what else to do. What do you want me to do?

> *(On the balcony,* **MARJORIE** *stands up quickly and staggers...)*

MORRIS. Easy now.

(...*Falling into* **MORRIS**' *arms. He resumes singing, now crooning, almost Crosby-like.*)

MORRIS.

THIS OLD MAN, HE PLAYED SEVEN,
HE PLAYED KNICK-KNACK UP IN HEAVEN...

(*On the beach:*)

LUTHER. Go inside. Leave me alone, I'll be there in a minute.

WALTER. Buddy, if you don't walk in that house with me right now I am going to pick up the phone and call the police, and they are going to come here and they are going to take you home. Because that is the only option you're giving me. Is that what you want?

LUTHER. I'll come.

WALTER. Thank you.

LUTHER. Just let me finish the seaweed.

WALTER. I'm sorry.

LUTHER. Please, Walter.

WALTER. We'll come back another day, when there aren't so many people –

LUTHER. I said we can go home. Did you hear me?

WALTER. I'm going to count to ten. And you'd better be inside by the time I'm done. One...

LUTHER. I just need to finish this first!

WALTER. Two...three...

LUTHER. I need to finish.

(**WALTER** *exits.* **MARJORIE** *is now half-conscious in* **MORRIS**' *arms as he sings and sways her back and forth.*)

MORRIS.

THIS OLD MAN, HE PLAYED NINE –

WALTER. (*Offstage.*) Four...

LUTHER. Walter?

WALTER. (*Offstage.*) Five...

LUTHER. I need to ask you something!

MARJORIE. Luther?

WALTER. *(Offstage.)* You know what to do, Luther. Six.

MORRIS. Where?

MARJORIE. Down there.

LUTHER. Come here!

WALTER. *(Offstage.)* Seven...

MORRIS. Luther!

LUTHER. Marjorie?

WALTER. *(Offstage.)* Eight...

> (**MORRIS** *waves to* **LUTHER. MARJORIE** *passes out in* **MORRIS'** *arms.)*

LUTHER. Marjorie!

WALTER. *(Offstage.)* Eight and a half...

> (**LUTHER** *scales the side of the building.)*

MORRIS. Where'd he go?

WALTER. Nine...

MORRIS. Marjorie?

WALTER. Nine and a half...

> (**WALTER** *returns to the beach, looking for* **LUTHER.***)*

Luther?!

> (**WALTER** *runs off toward the water.* **LUTHER** *jumps onto the balcony, facing* **MORRIS,** *who is holding* **MARJORIE.***)*

MORRIS. Hello there. My name is Morris.

> (**LUTHER** *makes a beeline for* **MORRIS,** *who recoils, screaming.)*

Scene Three

(A holding cell. **LUTHER** *sits, wearing his suit pants and shirt. His hands are cuffed to a heavy chain that is bolted to the floor.)*

(The door opens and **MARJORIE** *and* **WALTER** *are led into the room by* **CAPTAIN JAMES**.*)

MARJORIE. Oh my god.

WALTER. *(To* **CAPTAIN JAMES**.*)* I'm so sorry. Thank you.

CAPTAIN JAMES. No problem.

MARJORIE. Is this necessary? You have to chain him up like this?

WALTER. Marjorie –

CAPTAIN JAMES. I'm afraid so, ma'am.

> *(***MARJORIE*** *goes to* **LUTHER**.*)*

WALTER. We are so, so, so very sorry.

MARJORIE. *(To* **LUTHER***, scolding.)* What's wrong with you?

WALTER. What a blunder. Just a terrible mistake, the whole night.

MARJORIE. Is that blood? Are you bleeding?

WALTER. He's bleeding?

MARJORIE. Open your mouth.

> *(***MARJORIE*** *tries to inspect* **LUTHER***'s mouth, but he won't let her.)*

CAPTAIN JAMES. Ma'am?

WALTER. Oh, it's okay. He loves people. As long as he knows you.

MARJORIE. This never happens.

WALTER. Nothing like this has ever happened before.

MARJORIE. He would never do anything to hurt us.

WALTER. He didn't do anything to you, did he?

CAPTAIN JAMES. No, sir.

WALTER. Thank god. He really is the kindest soul you ever met. He makes birthday cards from scratch, he loves radio.

MARJORIE. He's just a boy.

WALTER. And we're usually very, very careful with him.

CAPTAIN JAMES. Of course.

WALTER. If anything, we're overprotective.

MARJORIE. We never let him go out alone.

WALTER. *(Aside, to* **CAPTAIN JAMES**.*)* We live in the ghetto.

CAPTAIN JAMES. Uh-huh.

WALTER. And he has a past.

CAPTAIN JAMES. I saw that. Six years in the army, huh?

WALTER. The nightmares.

CAPTAIN JAMES. Tremors?

WALTER. Terrible.

CAPTAIN JAMES. I can imagine.

MARJORIE. *(Pointedly.)* Can you? Can you really?

WALTER. *(After an awkward moment.)* We want to thank you again, Captain James, for letting us be here with him.

CAPTAIN JAMES. Well, we like to get the families together as soon as possible. It's stressful, we know, but it's an important part of the process.

MARJORIE. Luther, please open your mouth. Luther?

WALTER. *(Firm but pleading.)* Open your mouth!

(**LUTHER** *opens his mouth.)*

MARJORIE. He's bleeding.

WALTER. Jesus Christ. Is he okay?

MARJORIE. I think so. Are you okay?

LUTHER. I'm fine.

(**CAPTAIN JAMES** *offers* **MARJORIE** *a handkerchief.)*

CAPTAIN JAMES. I did two tours myself.

(*Begrudgingly,* **MARJORIE** *accepts the handkerchief and uses it to dab at* **LUTHER***'s mouth.)*

And if you don't mind me asking...

WALTER. Not at all, please, what else can we tell you?

CAPTAIN JAMES. Whereabouts in the ghetto do you all live?

WALTER. *(Wasn't expecting that.)* Down by the docks.

CAPTAIN JAMES. Near the abandoned factories?

WALTER. Yeah, on the other side of the projects.

CAPTAIN JAMES. Are you kidding? I love it down there. My girlfriend and I ride our horses over there almost every weekend.

MARJORIE. *(Aside, to* **LUTHER.***)* Oh, great.

LUTHER. *(Aside, to* **MARJORIE.***)* Horse people.

CAPTAIN JAMES. That's really an up-and-coming neighborhood, don't you think?

WALTER. We love it.

CAPTAIN JAMES. And it feels safe, right, like surprisingly so.

WALTER. Oh, yes.

MARJORIE. *(Can't believe* **WALTER***'s saying this.)* When it's light out.

WALTER. It's definitely a lot safer than it was a few years ago.

CAPTAIN JAMES. I heard there used to be packs of wild dogs down there.

WALTER. Oh, it's much better now.

MARJORIE. During the daytime.

CAPTAIN JAMES. And as far as the available housing –

MARJORIE. Not good.

WALTER. Well, now and then you hear of something.

MARJORIE. I haven't heard of anything in a long time.

WALTER. I still hear of something now and then.

CAPTAIN JAMES. Gosh, well, before you leave, maybe I can give you my card?

WALTER. Absolutely –

CAPTAIN JAMES. And that way if you do hear of anything –

WALTER. You'll be the first person we call.

> *(There's a knock at the door.)*

CAPTAIN JAMES. Yeah?

> *(The door opens. A puppet* **OFFICER** *sticks his head in the room.)*

OFFICER. Okay, Cap.

CAPTAIN JAMES. Be right there.

> (*The* **OFFICER** *leaves, closing the door behind him.*)

All right, folks, I'm going to go down the hall to check in with Mr. McHenry and his advocate, Ms. Liebowitz.

MARJORIE. *(Genuinely concerned.)* How is Mr. McHenry?

CAPTAIN JAMES. Well, I think he was a bit shaken up, to be honest.

MARJORIE. Of course.

CAPTAIN JAMES. But for a guy who just got bit in the face, I'd say he's doing pretty well.

MARJORIE. But he wasn't seriously injured?

CAPTAIN JAMES. I mean, he was bit in the face, so, I'm not sure what your definition of serious is. He had stitches, and they'll probably give him some powerful pain medication –

MARJORIE. But there isn't any permanent damage, is what I'm asking.

CAPTAIN JAMES. I still remember getting dumped in the second grade, Mrs. Forman. You know? It's just hard to say with these things.

MARJORIE. May I speak with him?

CAPTAIN JAMES. That's what I'm going to find out. Here's how it works. He makes a statement, we write that up. He meets with Ms. Liebowitz in private – that's what he's been doing – and she helps him decide if he wants to press charges.

WALTER. Charges?

MARJORIE. What charges? He's going to press charges?

CAPTAIN JAMES. Hopefully not. They rarely do on my shift, and I get fifteen vets a month in here. But that is Mr. McHenry's right if he so chooses. Now, hopefully, Ms. Liebowitz has done her job beautifully, and Mr. McHenry has come to understand that a long and costly court trial is not in anyone's interests. Hopefully, he will decline to press charges and opt instead to take part in the VCRP. What is the VCRP? The Veteran's Conflict Resolution Program, or VCRP, which I myself helped to develop, is something we do right here in this room, and it has five components. Part One – Mr. McHenry is given the opportunity to address Luther, and to say whatever he needs to say about this evening's unfortunate events. Part Two – Luther is given the opportunity to apologize to Mr. McHenry for all the pain and suffering he has caused. Part Three – Mr. McHenry is given the opportunity to grant Luther his legally binding forgiveness. Part Four – Mr. and Mrs. Forman are given the opportunity to offer a small token of appreciation to Mr. McHenry. Now, this transaction is strictly off the record, and state law prohibits me from making any suggestion about what the size of that gift – in the event that there is one – should be. However, I can tell you that some previous parents have given something on the order of fifteen to twenty-five hundred dollars. Okay? And finally, Part Five – the bread and butter of my life in law enforcement: paperwork. And that's it. That's the whole thing. If we can make it through those five easy steps – and most of the time we can – the matter is resolved right here, and nobody has to go before a judge or jury. Why do we do this, you may ask. We do it because the judicial system is challenged. We do it because the courts don't give a rat's tail about people like Luther, and because, in my experience, this is the fairest and fastest way to reach a just outcome for everyone.

WALTER. What happens if Mr. McHenry decides to press charges?

CAPTAIN JAMES. Then the case goes to court. And if Luther lucks out and gets acquitted, which does happen, then he can go home a free man. And if not, then he will be put down.

(*After a moment.*)

Does anyone have other questions?

(A moment.)

I'll go talk to Mr. McHenry.

*(**CAPTAIN JAMES** exits. It's quiet.)*

WALTER. We should try to be nice.

MARJORIE. I agree.

WALTER. To the police officer.

MARJORIE. Right. But just to him, right?

WALTER. To everyone, and especially to him.

MARJORIE. *(After a moment.)* I'm sorry I didn't invite Captain James to come live with us.

WALTER. Wow. That's perfect.

MARJORIE. From now on I will try to be a better salesperson for our neighborhood so that everyone and their girlfriends *and* their horses wants to move there and we have to move somewhere else.

LUTHER. How about Mississippi?

WALTER. I am trying to establish a rapport with a man who might hold Luther's fate in his hands.

MARJORIE. I know. You're just being nice. That's what you do when you want to get something out of someone.

WALTER. Is this how you take responsibility for what happened tonight?

MARJORIE. And there it is. There it is.

WALTER. Yes, it is.

MARJORIE. I knew it was coming.

WALTER. And here it is.

MARJORIE. When you were being so sweet on the way over here, and holding my hand in the waiting room, I knew it was all just a cover for the onslaught of blame that would soon be catapulting my way.

WALTER. And here it is.

LUTHER. Guys?

WALTER. Where were you, Marjorie?

MARJORIE. Where was I? I was at *your* party.

WALTER. No, where were you? I was at that party, and I didn't see you all night.

MARJORIE. Because I was busy: being nice! Mingling with your co-workers, just like you asked me to do. And look where it got us.

WALTER. Are you...? Hold on. Is there some small possibility that you are blaming me for this disaster?

MARJORIE. What I'm saying, Walter, if you would listen, is that I don't think we should be blaming anyone.

WALTER. But I want to. I want to blame you.

MARJORIE. *(Sincere, accepting responsibility.)* Okay then: blame me.

WALTER. I am! Do you see my head? Do you know what's going on inside of it? You are being blamed.

MARJORIE. And deservedly so.

WALTER. Who wanted to bring him to the party in the first place?

MARJORIE. I did.

WALTER. Who swore up and down that this is what Luther needed, and promised to keep an eye on him all night long?

MARJORIE. I did. He wanted to go off and talk to people. He wanted to have a little bit of human interaction, and I wanted that for him too. I should have said no.

WALTER. That's right.

MARJORIE. And instead I gave him the same advice you gave me, and sent him on his way.

WALTER. What advice? You're always talking about these waves of unsolicited advice that I'm always giving you. So tell me, Marjorie, what was this mysterious advice?

MARJORIE. Just be your kind, wonderful self. Remember that other people are just as nervous and insecure as you are and try to take care of them, and everything will turn out fine.

WALTER. But that... I didn't... That was a *suggestion*. And it wasn't intended for Luther.

LUTHER. Why not?

WALTER. Because. You and Marjorie are different.

LUTHER. So are you and Marjorie.

WALTER. Yes, we're all different.

LUTHER. But you decided that if it worked for you, it would work for her too.

MARJORIE. Right.

LUTHER. But not for me.

WALTER. *(Caught, changing the subject.)* And I know that you two didn't just eat cereal today!

MARJORIE. Excuse me?

WALTER. Are you familiar with the phrase "peanut butter and chocolate ice cream," Marjorie? Yes, I think you are. All too familiar.
(To **LUTHER,** *composing himself again.)* Of course it could work for you, buddy, to be that way with people. In the right environment.

LUTHER. Like, at home.

WALTER. Sure.

LUTHER. Or in prison.

WALTER. No, what? Is that...?

MARJORIE. Honey? Do you think of our home as being a prison?

LUTHER. I understand what you're saying, Walt. You don't trust me.

WALTER. No. That's not it, buddy. It's the world that I don't trust.

LUTHER. See, I trust the world but not myself.

WALTER. How could you, after all you've been through, still have trust in the world?

LUTHER. It's consistent. It knows what it wants and sticks to its guns. But me? Who am I going to be five minutes from now? I don't know. Do you?

MARJORIE. Honey, what happened tonight when I left you alone?

LUTHER. I had a nice talk with a doctor.

MARJORIE. You did? Well, that's wonderful.

WALTER. Buddy, that's great.

MARJORIE. What'd you guys talk about?

LUTHER. Art, women, war.

WALTER. Sounds a lot more interesting than any conversation I had.

MARJORIE. Is he someone you might want to socialize with again?

LUTHER. I don't think so.

MARJORIE. Because we could probably track him down and arrange some kind of –

LUTHER. No thank you.

WALTER. *(After a moment.)* Luther, I'm sorry I got so worked up out on the beach.

LUTHER. I was out of line.

WALTER. I could've handled it differently.

LUTHER. You were trying to make things better.

MARJORIE. And I'm sorry that I left you alone for so long.

LUTHER. Yeah, that probably wasn't the best decision. But it was the fun one. Who was that man you were talking to?

MARJORIE. Morris. He works with Walter.

WALTER. And tell me again, what does he do?

MARJORIE. Business operations.

LUTHER. You talked to him all night?

MARJORIE. Well, except for when we were dancing. He really is an interesting man, Walter, so different from those other people you work with.

WALTER. I didn't even know we had a business operations.

LUTHER. You were dancing?

MARJORIE. *(To* **LUTHER.***)* Yeah, we're the ones who got the whole thing started.

(To **WALTER.***)* He said that you'd met but you might not remember.

LUTHER. Is that why he was holding you? Because you were dancing?

MARJORIE. No, he was holding me because...well, I'd had a bit too much to drink and wasn't feeling so hot, but thankfully Morris was there to help.

WALTER. Were you sick?

MARJORIE. A little bit.

WALTER. Like, barfy?

MARJORIE. Maybe.

WALTER. Oh, Margie.

(**WALTER** *comforts her.*)

MARJORIE. I feel better now.

WALTER. I can't believe you two were off making friends just as I was figuring out how little I like everybody I work with.

MARJORIE. What? Why?

WALTER. You can't have a real conversation with those people. Either it's this ridiculous game of dueling checklists or some kind of nonsensical verbal beach ball, or else it's just ass-kissing, which I don't like in myself and I really don't like in them.

MARJORIE. You're not like that, Walter, and neither is Morris. I know you two are going to hit it off.

LUTHER. He was trying to hurt you.

MARJORIE. No, honey. He wasn't.

LUTHER. He was squeezing you, I saw it.

MARJORIE. He was helping me stand up.

LUTHER. You were too sick to notice.

MARJORIE. Notice what?

LUTHER. You were drunk. She was drunk.

MARJORIE. Luther, I know you were just trying to protect me.

LUTHER. You're probably still drunk right now.

MARJORIE. I am not.

LUTHER. He put his hands inside of her.

MARJORIE. Stop it!

WALTER. I think – and I may be wrong here, but I think – we all got just a little bit overtired tonight. That's what I think.

MARJORIE. *(To LUTHER.)* You have every right to be angry at me, but you do not have the right to be mean.

WALTER. *(Moving on.)* So we think of this Morris person as a pretty fair-minded guy?

MARJORIE. Yes.

WALTER. Someday we might even all be friends?

MARJORIE. Well, I would hope so.

WALTER. And so given that, what do we think we should offer? As far as this gift the captain is talking about.

MARJORIE. I don't have any idea. I don't imagine that he would take anything.

WALTER. No?

MARJORIE. I mean, we wouldn't take money from some vet's family just because of a stupid accident, would we?

WALTER. No, I don't think so, but that's us. But you seem to be saying that Morris is a lot like us?

MARJORIE. He is. Philosophically.

WALTER. So…?

MARJORIE. There's no way he expects us to offer him twenty-five hundred dollars.

WALTER. Right. Unless that's what Captain James told him to expect.

MARJORIE. Do we have twenty-five hundred dollars?

WALTER. I would say we have thirty-one hundred dollars.

MARJORIE. In total?

WALTER. Not including our debt.

MARJORIE. All right. Here's what we do. We offer him two thousand dollars. And he probably turns us down, but if not, then at most he takes fifteen hundred.

WALTER. And if he turns us down flat, should we assume he's just doing that to be polite but that really he's expecting us to insist and give him something regardless?

MARJORIE. Well, we could make him dinner.

WALTER. I'm sure we could.

MARJORIE. Oh, just say what you want to give him, Walter!

WALTER. I don't want to give him anything! I want to give him exactly enough to make him happy, so that you and I and Luther can all go home tonight. Whatever that is. Whatever you think that is.

MARJORIE. *(Considers.)* We offer him two. If he takes it, fine. And if he says he doesn't want it, then we accept his answer, give him our heartfelt thanks and call it a day.

WALTER. Okay.

MARJORIE. You can live with that?

WALTER. Yes.

MARJORIE. Now, if we do end up paying him two grand...we might have to cut back on some things as a family.

WALTER. Like what?

MARJORIE. Takeout food?

WALTER. We won't order in as often.

MARJORIE. No. We won't order in at all.

WALTER. Oh. Okay. Okay. Well, and this is something I've been thinking about for awhile anyway, but: I don't need to have cable.

MARJORIE. Are you sure?

WALTER. Yes.

MARJORIE. All right. And I'll see if I can sell off our theater tickets.

WALTER. That would be great.

MARJORIE. And I'll cancel the weekend edition of the paper.

WALTER. No –

MARJORIE. Yes, it's fine.

WALTER. But honey, you need that.

MARJORIE. No, I don't. I don't.

WALTER. I'm going to buy – do you know what I'm going to do? I'm going to buy one of those ten-pound bags of coffee, wholesale, and then we can just keep it in the freezer through winter. And I want to start buying wine by the case. Did you know you get ten to fifteen percent off that way?

MARJORIE. On different bottles of wine?

WALTER. Yeah.

MARJORIE. I thought it all had to be the same kind.

WALTER. No, you can make it different bottles, we just tell them what we want.

MARJORIE. Do you think the three of us can be trusted with having a case-full of wine in the apartment?

WALTER. It's either that or we start buying it by the jug.

MARJORIE. From now on we only have wine *with* dinner.

WALTER. Ow. Okay, I can commit to that.

MARJORIE. And I'm going to look into getting Luther's meds from Canada.

WALTER. Honey, that's brilliant.

MARJORIE. As long as it's legitimate.

WALTER. And I'll do the research.

MARJORIE. I don't mind doing it –

WALTER. But you're swamped at home. I'm the one with the job. We have to start taking advantage of my free time.

MARJORIE. I'll tell you one thing though: I'm finally going to get some of those green refrigerator bags for the vegetables.

WALTER. I remember you talking about those.

MARJORIE. You just wash 'em out and reuse 'em.

WALTER. I mean that's good for us and the environment. We should do that no matter what.

MARJORIE. And I am going to work extra hard to get some new clients.

WALTER. Honey, you already work extra hard.

MARJORIE. It isn't enough.

LUTHER. Why don't you cancel your vacation?

WALTER. No. You need that trip, Marjorie. And so do I. This family needs you and me to take that trip together.

MARJORIE. We'll see. We'll see.

(Keys rattle at the door. **CAPTAIN JAMES** *enters with* **MORRIS**, *his cheek heavily bandaged, and* **MS. LIEBOWITZ**, *a puppet in a pantsuit.* **LUTHER** *retreats, moving off by himself.)*

CAPTAIN JAMES. Hello, hello. And how's everybody doing in here?

(It's quiet.)

Well. Mr. and Mrs. Forman, Luther, this is Ms. Liebowitz.

MS. LIEBOWITZ. Sandy.

CAPTAIN JAMES. And I believe you all know Mr. McHenry.

WALTER. Walter.

CAPTAIN JAMES. Oh, I thought you two worked together.

WALTER. It's a big company.

MARJORIE. Hello Morris.

MORRIS. Hello Marjorie. How are you?

MARJORIE. Oh Morris, I'm fine. Are you okay?

MORRIS. *(Fighting back tears.)* He bit my face.

MARJORIE. I know. And I am so sorry. Can I give you a hug?

MORRIS. *(Backing off, consulting* **MS. LIEBOWITZ**.*)* Uh...

MS. LIEBOWITZ. Maybe we should take this one step at a time –

MORRIS. Yeah –

CAPTAIN JAMES. That might be best.

MARJORIE. Yes, of course.

MS. LIEBOWITZ. Is this Luther? Luther? Hi, Luther. I'm Sandy.

LUTHER. Hello Sandy.

MS. LIEBOWITZ. I understand you had a rough night tonight.

LUTHER. Yes.

MS. LIEBOWITZ. Well, who among us hasn't had one of those? And I mean recently, you know what I'm saying? You know, whenever it happens to me, all I can do is think, gosh, I wish that didn't happen. And then about five seconds later I think, oh, I wish I could make it unhappen. And then I realize I can't, so I mope around feeling sorry for myself for as long as I can – you give me a month and I'll fill it, with Thin Mints, if possible – until I have to try to move on. Because that's what we do, isn't it, weird little creatures that we are? And that's why I'm here tonight, Luther. To help all of us try to move on. Is it okay with you, and everyone else, if I do that?

WALTER, MARJORIE, LUTHER & MORRIS. *(Overlapping.)* Yes.

MS. LIEBOWITZ. Good. I have only one recommendation as we move forward, and that's this, and you can feel free to ignore it if you like, but I say: If the seas get rough, look to the horizon. That's it, that's all I got. So, Morris, do you have some things, some thoughts and feelings that you would like to share with Luther?

MORRIS. Yes.

MS. LIEBOWITZ. Beautiful. And Luther, do you feel up to letting Morris talk a little bit about his thoughts and feelings?

LUTHER. Yes.

MS. LIEBOWITZ. Wunderbar.

(*To* **CAPTAIN JAMES.***)* I may catch the 12:36 train yet.

(*To* **MORRIS.***)* Morris? Whenever you're ready.

MORRIS. Uh…hello, Luther.

LUTHER. Hello.

MORRIS. *(To* **MS. LIEBOWITZ.***)* Is he allowed to talk?

MS. LIEBOWITZ. No. Luther, while Morris is speaking, your job is just to stand there and listen. Really try to just listen. Even if Morris asks you a question or gives you the impression that he wants you to say something in return, you just stay quiet, okay? And then you remember that thing for later so you can bring it up when it's your turn. Does that make sense?

LUTHER. Yes.

MORRIS. That's talking.

WALTER. Jesus Christ –

MS. LIEBOWITZ. Morris, when I am speaking to Luther, he is allowed to speak to me in return, okay?

MORRIS. Okay.

MS. LIEBOWITZ. And Mr. and Mrs. Forman, if you could just remind yourselves of the same thing. We really encourage everyone, no matter how tempted you may be to interject, to speak only when it's your turn.

CAPTAIN JAMES. Everyone needs to know that when they have the floor, it's theirs, and nobody else is going to take it away from them. Sandy?

MS. LIEBOWITZ. Thank you, Captain James –

CAPTAIN JAMES. We don't want any of you to look back on this night in years to come and say, "Oh, I just wish that I'd said that one other thing."

MS. LIEBOWITZ. Is everyone ready?

MARJORIE. Yes but, I'm sorry, could I ask just one stupid thing before we continue? Don't we need an advocate for Luther?

MS. LIEBOWITZ. Captain James?

CAPTAIN JAMES. You're more than welcome to hire one, Mrs. Forman. But the state cannot provide one for you. The state will provide an attorney for a defense at trial. If you want to go that route, you may, or if you want to bring somebody in to guide you through this process, we can hold Luther as long as you need us to. I would caution that most attorneys will push toward a trial because that's what attorneys do. But the choice is yours.

MS. LIEBOWITZ. And I should add that while technically I am Morris' advocate – and I told Morris this earlier – I'm not on anyone's side. I just want to see everyone get home so we can all get on to our next big booboos in life.

> (**WALTER, MARJORIE,** *and* **LUTHER** *all share a look. It's understood that they want to move forward.*)

MS. LIEBOWITZ. Morris, the floor is yours.

MORRIS. Okay.

    (Considers.)

Can I see how long the chain is?

WALTER. Are you kidding me?

CAPTAIN JAMES. Shhh.

MS. LIEBOWITZ. Luther, could you please show Morris how long the chain is.

    *(**LUTHER** walks toward **MORRIS**, who backs away, but the chain stops **LUTHER** short of him.)*

MORRIS. Okay. You can go back. Tell him to go back –

WALTER. Hey, you can't –

CAPTAIN JAMES. Mr. Forman –

MARJORIE. Honey –

WALTER. He can't talk to him like that –

CAPTAIN JAMES. You have to let us do our job.

    *(**LUTHER** walks back to the corner of the cell.)*

MORRIS. Excuse me if I seem nervous. It's hard to explain how unsafe you can feel after something like this. I'm sure I'll be one hundred percent better in just a few days, but right now I don't even want to go to the bathroom by myself. I don't want to go to another party as long as I live.

    (Clears his throat.)

Marjorie, I had a lot of fun with you. You are very kind, and no matter what you say, I know that you're a great parent. And wife. I think you're probably the most sensitive person I've ever met, and I hope we can still be friends.

    *(**MARJORIE** mouths "Me too.")*

MS. LIEBOWITZ. *(After a long moment.)* Morris, is there anything you want to say to Luther?

MORRIS. Yes. Luther, I really didn't like what you did to me tonight. It hurt me a lot.

It feels like I have a piece of glass in my face. I think it was very, very nice of Marjorie and Walter to take you in and share their life with you – I bet you get more love in one day than some people get in a lifetime. Which is something you should think about. It was extremely terrible of you to betray Walter and Marjorie's trust. And it was very, very bad of you to attack me, an innocent man, in the middle of a very fun party. I know you don't get out much, but I wish you knew, I really wish you knew how many bad parties the average person has to go to before they get to a fun one. This was my most fun night this year. And you ruined it. I know, Luther, that you have had a hard life. But so have I. Look at me. Life is hard. The difference between you and me, Luther, is that I am not a bastard animal.

WALTER. Hey –

MORRIS. Shut up! Okay, Walter? Just listen to what they told you to do and be quiet for once. Not everything is all about you.

(After a moment.)

Luther, I think you are the worst kind of violent animal there is. You are the same kind of animal who tormented me my whole life. Ever since I was little. Ever since Darryl Shanley decided it was cool to punch me hard, in the arm, every day at recess, violent, disgusting animals like you have taken pleasure in making me suffer. Why? Because you could. Because you're strong and I'm weak. And whatever happened to you in the war doesn't matter. That's important. You can't blame this on the war. We would not even have any wars if bastard animals like you weren't around to fight them. I would never harm another person. Do you know that about me?

I would rather die than kill or beat another man, and that's what makes me human. But you would do any of those things, and that's what makes you you. Not the victim. I am the victim. We are all victims of animals like you. You should see how hard it is to be the way we are. Some day. You should try to be more like us.

MS. LIEBOWITZ. All right. Luther? Is there anything you would like to say to Mr. McHenry?

LUTHER. *(Considers.)* I'm sorry.

MORRIS. *(Considers.)* I forgive you.

MS. LIEBOWITZ. Beautiful.

　　　　*(***MORRIS** *goes quickly to embrace* **LUTHER.***)*

CAPTAIN JAMES. *(Warning against it.)* Sir?

MS. LIEBOWITZ. And is that really a good idea? Maybe it is.

　　　　*(***LUTHER** *puts his shackled arms around* **MORRIS** *and embraces him in return.* **CAPTAIN JAMES** *approaches, keys jangling.)*

CAPTAIN JAMES. If I may...

　　　　*(***LUTHER** *raises his arms so that* **MORRIS** *can step away.)*

　　　　*(***CAPTAIN JAMES** *unlocks* **LUTHER***'s shackles.)*

How's that?

LUTHER. Better.

　　　　*(***MORRIS** *turns to* **MARJORIE.***)*

MORRIS. Marjorie –

MARJORIE. *(Foaming with rage.)* We would like...

MORRIS. Yes?

MARJORIE. Mr. McHenry?

MORRIS. Morris.

MARJORIE. We want to give you our money.

MORRIS. What?

MARJORIE. Everything we have, which is...

WALTER. Thirty-one –

MARJORIE. Thirty-one hundred dollars.

MORRIS. No –

MARJORIE. Yes, all of it –

MORRIS. But I don't want it –

MS. LIEBOWITZ. I don't think Mrs. Forman means –

MARJORIE. Don't tell me what I mean! That is what we have and we want you to take it, every cent. Isn't that right, Walter?

WALTER. Yes.

MARJORIE. And then you will never have to hear from us again.

MORRIS. But that's not what I wanted.

MARJORIE. And I will never have to look into your hateful eyes again. And you will never, ever, say another word about – not one more word – about my son ever again.

WALTER. Will you take a check?

MORRIS. *(To* **MS. LIEBOWITZ.***)* You told me to say what I felt –

MS. LIEBOWITZ. That's right –

WALTER. I'll write you a check –

MORRIS. She told me –

MS. LIEBOWITZ. And you did a terrific job.

WALTER. Who has a pen?

MORRIS. I don't want your money –

CAPTAIN JAMES. Why don't we all cool off for a moment.

MARJORIE. Write him a check, Walter.

WALTER. Anyone have a pen?

MS. LIEBOWITZ. It's better to get these things out in the open.

CAPTAIN JAMES. Sandy?

WALTER. I need a pen.

CAPTAIN JAMES. Maybe we could try to de-escalate?

MS. LIEBOWITZ. I know how to do my job, Elliot –

WALTER. A pen?

CAPTAIN JAMES. Your job doesn't include rushing to catch a train, Sandy –

MORRIS. I don't want your filthy money!

> (**WALTER** *goes after* **MORRIS**, *grabbing him by the lapel.*)

WALTER. Who cares what you want?!

CAPTAIN JAMES. No!

WALTER. Who cares?!

MARJORIE. Walter!

MORRIS. Go ahead!

MS. LIEBOWITZ. Hey, hey, hey!

MORRIS. *(Barely able to breathe.)* Does it make you feel better?

> *(**CAPTAIN JAMES** tries to pull **WALTER** off of **MORRIS**, but **WALTER** wraps his legs around **MORRIS**'s middle. **MARJORIE** and **MS. LIEBOWITZ** try to separate the men, but still **WALTER** won't loosen his grip, and **MORRIS** refuses to defend himself.)*

Does it make you feel like a man?

> *(**CAPTAIN JAMES** yanks **WALTER** away, but **WALTER** lunges at **MORRIS** again. This time **CAPTAIN JAMES** grabs **WALTER**'s thumb and brings him to his knees with a military move designed to instantly incapacitate.)*

> *(**LUTHER**, seeing **WALTER** in peril, grabs **CAPTAIN JAMES** from behind and breaks his neck, killing him.)*

> *(**LUTHER** gently lays **CAPTAIN JAMES** on the ground.)*

Does it make you feel like a man?

> *(It's quiet.)*

> *(**MS. LIEBOWITZ** goes to **CAPTAIN JAMES**.)*

MS. LIEBOWITZ. Elliot? Oh dear.

> *(**LUTHER** goes to the shackles, puts them on, and locks them.)*

Scene Four

> *(Marjorie and Walter's apartment.* **WALTER**, *unkempt, sits on the couch in sweatpants, a wrinkled shirt, socks, and sandals. There's a manila folder on the couch next to him.)*

> *(***MARJORIE**, *wearing a corporate suit, mills around the apartment – anything not to sit down. Both drink wine.)*

> *(Through a speakerphone that* **WALTER** *has set next to him on the couch, we hear* **LUTHER**, *whom we also see, in prison.)*

LUTHER. So Houston goes up to Shrub, he's sitting at the end of the dining hall, and he goes, "Hey Shrub. You think I'm pretty?"

WALTER. Uh-huh?

MARJORIE. Shrub's the one you knew from before?

WALTER. No, that's Archie.

LUTHER. You're thinking of Archie. He got transferred.

MARJORIE. Transferred?

> *(***WALTER** *mimes someone getting a lethal injection.)*

LUTHER. Shrub's the one who killed his C.O. because the guy kept taking away his leave?

MARJORIE. Okay.

WALTER. And what did Shrub say when Houston asked him that?

LUTHER. I don't know. By the time I could hear what was happening, Houston had gone down the row asking fifteen other guys the same question. "Hey, so-and-so, you think I'm pretty?" And everyone made up something: "Yeah," or "Why not?"; a couple guys even said "No." But you couldn't just not answer, right?

WALTER. Right?

LUTHER. When he got to me, I was like, "Houston, I think you're lovely." I don't know where that came from.

WALTER. Genius.

LUTHER. Mostly everyone was just staring at their food and mumbling, because they all knew – because Houston is messed up; I mean, we have guards in here who won't look that guy in the eye – no matter what you said, you were taking your life in your hands, right? And every time he asked, the suspense just kept building, and so finally he gets to this kid Palacek, right? And Palacek didn't even serve, he's just some street punk. And Houston gets in his face and he goes, "Hey, Palacek, you think I'm pretty?" And the whole dining room goes quiet. 'Cause we can smell it, you know? Palacek's the one. And Palacek goes, "Uh, sure, Houston." Just like that.

WALTER. Right?

LUTHER. And Houston looks at him for a second and then he goes, "Oh. Because I think you're the ugliest motherfucker I've ever seen."

WALTER. *(Laughing big.)* Bah!

LUTHER. And then he walks away.

WALTER. Come on! That is good.

LUTHER. We thought so. Even Palacek was laughing. You should see him now, he's all proud, like he accomplished something.

WALTER. You guys really have a tight bond in there, don't you?

LUTHER. *(Not really.)* Yeah.

MARJORIE. Honey, what did they give you for lunch today?

LUTHER. Today? Let's see. Today we had slop and a roll.

MARJORIE. And what exactly is slop again, that's like a soup?

LUTHER. Not exactly.

WALTER. It's more like a stew.

LUTHER. No, it's more like a slop. Sort of like what we used to make papier-mâché with, only tangier. What about you guys, what did you have for lunch today?

WALTER. I had chili.

LUTHER. Nice, you made chili?

WALTER. *(A touch embarrassed.)* From a can.

LUTHER. Hey, nothing wrong with chili from a can. You crumble up some chips to go on top?

WALTER. *(Rebounding.)* I did crumble up a few chips to go on top.

LUTHER. Nice. And Marjorie, what about you?

MARJORIE. I had a salad in the cafeteria.

LUTHER. And how was that?

MARJORIE. Well, I ate the whole thing.

LUTHER. That's what matters. You got to keep eating, right?

MARJORIE. Yup.

LUTHER. The job's working out okay?

MARJORIE. Yeah, you know. It's different.

LUTHER. Have you made any friends?

MARJORIE. There are people I'm friendly with.

LUTHER. Uh-huh. And do you talk to those people?

MARJORIE. Yes, Luther, I talk to the people at my work.

LUTHER. Well, that's all you can do, right?

WALTER. *(Patting the folder.)* I got some good news.

LUTHER. Yeah?

WALTER. About the case. A very interesting piece of information.

MARJORIE. Walter –

LUTHER. What case?

WALTER. Against McHenry. So get this: not only did this fraud never work for my company, but it turns out he's done the same thing on at least two other occasions.

LUTHER. Done what?

WALTER. Lied his way into a corporate event. For a company that did not employ him.

LUTHER. Is that a crime?

MARJORIE. In Walter's eyes, it is.

WALTER. In the eyes of the law it is! It's called felony impersonation. It's a Class Six felony. On top of trespassing, which is a Class B misdemeanor. He can get jail time, Lu.

LUTHER. But why?

WALTER. Why?

LUTHER. Why do you want to do that?

WALTER. Luther, if that man hadn't been at that party –

MARJORIE. For god's sake –

LUTHER. Walter –

WALTER. Doing something illegal and immoral –

LUTHER. Walter?

MARJORIE. He was trying to make friends –

WALTER. No, Marjorie, if you want to make friends, you crash the party of a rock band. You don't go sneaking into a corporate mixer! Which this guy did more than once. He needs to be punished.

MARJORIE. I'm not having this conversation.

LUTHER. He came to see me.

MARJORIE. Morris did?

WALTER. When?

LUTHER. Last week.

MARJORIE. And you're just telling us now?

LUTHER. I wanted to tell you –

MARJORIE. What was he doing there? Did he say why he came?

WALTER. *(To* **MARJORIE.***)* Why do you think? He was trying to get Luther to incriminate himself.

MARJORIE. Against what, he's already in jail?

WALTER. That's the case against Luther. How many times do I have to tell you, they're separate cases.

LUTHER. I asked him to come.

    (Silence.)

He doesn't look too good, you know? He's sort of shrinking.

MARJORIE. What's wrong with him?

LUTHER. He says he thinks he has something called fibromyalgia.

WALTER. Fibromy–?! It's not even a real disease!

LUTHER. Whatever it is, he's not doing too well.

MARJORIE. What did you tell him?

WALTER. You ask that jerk to come visit you, and you won't even let us –

LUTHER. It's different with you guys. I told you. It's too hard.

WALTER. To hell with hard.

MARJORIE. Walter, please.

WALTER. Fibromyalgia. He might as well say he got cooties.

MARJORIE. Honey, why did you want to see him?

LUTHER. I wanted him to know that I was a nice kid, and I never would've punched him in the arm.

    (A moment.)

And it's not like you stop being a person once you enlist, but the stuff they ask you to do, the stuff I did, that isn't person stuff. I mean some of it is, like directing traffic, but the rest... And once you do that stuff, that's you. That's who you are. I was talking to Archie before he got transferred, and I was saying just how it sucks that he wouldn't get another chance to do it right, and he said, "You know, Lu, if you kill a guy on the street, they don't ever call you an ex-murderer," right? "There's no such thing as being a former serial killer." And what he meant was...after you serve, they can do everything in the world for you, they can put you in the luckiest situation with the most wonderful people and they can fill your life with beauty and love until it's pouring out of your ears, but what are they going to do with that other part of you? The part that did that stuff? You see what I'm saying?

MARJORIE. You want us to think that you're not a human being, Luther?

LUTHER. I want you to know that it wasn't you. Or Morris or my family, and it wasn't even the army, okay? The army was just looking after itself. The reason I'm here is because of me.

MARJORIE. Honey, I'm sorry.

LUTHER. Don't be sorry –

MARJORIE. But I am, because I can't accept that. Baby, I deal with lots of people every day, and I can count on one hand the number who are half the human being you are. Whatever amazing qualities you possess –

LUTHER. Marjorie –

MARJORIE. Whatever darkness or anger is mixed in there with it, that is all part of the magic.

LUTHER. You're not listening –

MARJORIE. We let you down, Luther.

LUTHER. No –

MARJORIE. Yes, we did, I let you down. I was selfish and stupid –

LUTHER. It was my decision, Marjorie. Mine. What else can I say that about in my whole life? If I get nothing else being here, please give me that. Give me the respect as a man – I'm a grown man – to decide how I got here. I got me here. That's how it happened. And if you try to make me think otherwise, you will wreck my fucking heart.

WALTER. *(After a moment.)* Hey Lu?
I'm going to send you the file. Once I've collected all the info on McHenry, just so you can see the whole case. And if you don't want to do anything with it, we don't have to. Only if you want to.

LUTHER. Yeah. Okay.

    (After a moment.)

Any luck finding a job, Walt?

WALTER. Well, I have a few leads.

LUTHER. Yeah?

WALTER. Yeah. Don't want to jinx it, though.

LUTHER. Of course. It's all about timing with that sort of thing, right?

WALTER. Absolutely.

MARJORIE. Is there anything you need, honey? Anything you want us to send?

LUTHER. Nah, I don't think so, I'm good.

MARJORIE. Another book or some magazines?

LUTHER. You can send me some magazines. And some dope, if you have any. Just kidding. Not really.

WALTER. So, Lu –

LUTHER. Ah shit, that's the sign, I gotta go.

MARJORIE. *(Trying to keep him on the phone.)* And so, but, but...you didn't say what happened with the puzzles.

LUTHER. The what?

MARJORIE. The puzzles, you were going to see if they'd let you do puzzles?

LUTHER. Oh, yeah. They said no.

MARJORIE. You're kidding.

LUTHER. I gotta go, guys.

MARJORIE. Why not?

LUTHER. I love you.

WALTER & MARJORIE. Love you.

> *(A dial tone is heard. Lights on **LUTHER**.)*
>
> *(It's quiet for a long time.)*

MARJORIE. Is there any more wine?

WALTER. Should be.

> *(**WALTER** spots the jug of wine – it's empty.)*

I'll get some.

MARJORIE. I'll go.

WALTER. I'll go. You've been working all day.

MARJORIE. *(Wrapping herself in the blanket on the couch.)* Should I make us some dinner?

WALTER. Sure.

MARJORIE. Do we have anything?

WALTER. Uh...I think there might be some tuna in the cupboard.

MARJORIE. Okay.

WALTER. You want me to pick something up?

MARJORIE. No-no.

WALTER. *(Pats his pockets.)* Uh...hmm...money.

> (**MARJORIE** *digs out some money from her purse, gives it to him.*)

MARJORIE. If you do walk by the market and see something that inspires you...

WALTER. Such as?

MARJORIE. I don't know, whatever. Not chili.

WALTER. You want me to go shopping?

MARJORIE. No, just if you see something along the way.

WALTER. I don't know what that means.

MARJORIE. Just get wine.

> (**WALTER** *dons a beaten-up baseball cap. He goes to the door.*)

Aren't you going to be cold?

WALTER. I don't think so.

MARJORIE. Take a jacket.

WALTER. It doesn't look cold.

> (**WALTER** *goes to the closet, rifles through it.*)

You haven't seen my windbreaker, have you?

MARJORIE. No.

> (**WALTER** *pulls out a puffy, old winter parka.*)

WALTER. Remember this thing? I was wearing it when we picked him up.

> (**WALTER** *puts the coat on. It's a bit too tight.*)

Still fit?

> (**MARJORIE** *nods.*)

> (**WALTER** *puts his hand in the coat pocket and pulls out a yellow, folded-up piece of paper. He quickly stuffs it back into the pocket.*)

MARJORIE. What's that?

WALTER. Nothing.

> (**MARJORIE** *goes to him.*)

MARJORIE. Is that it? Is that Luther's profile?

WALTER. What?

> (**MARJORIE** *shoves her hand into* **WALTER**'s *coat pocket, grabbing at the paper.*)

What are you doing?

MARJORIE. Give it!

> (**MARJORIE** *snatches the paper away from him.*)

WALTER. What are you doing?

> (**MARJORIE** *goes to the couch and sits, clutching the paper.*)

> (**WALTER** *goes to the door, about to leave.*)

Were we the wonderful people? He said something about wonderful people.

> (*They look at each other.*)

> (**WALTER** *goes to join* **MARJORIE** *on the couch.*)

> (**MARJORIE** *unfolds the yellow piece of paper and* **WALTER** *looks at it, putting his arm around her. She grabs her reading glasses from the nightstand. Together they read.*)

The End